BATMAN™
&
ROBIN™

OFFICIAL ANNUAL

Grandreams
Children's Book Publishers

Published by
Grandreams Limited, 435-437 Edgware Road
Little Venice, London W2 1TH

Originally published in a different format by
Landoll, Inc. Ashland Ohio 44805 USA

Printed in Belgium

£5.75

Out of the darkness two powerful vehicles speed toward Gotham City.

Inside the sleek, black Batmobile, the man called Batman radios his young partner. "Ten police cruisers are frozen on the Gotham Expressway."

Robin reads the data on the console of his turbo-charged motorcycle, the Redbird. "And a giant drilling truck is burrowing under the city."

The crime fighters agree: "It's Mr. Freeze." Their computers show the cold criminal heading for the Gotham Museum—*where the Great White Diamond is on exhibit.*

At that moment, in the Gotham Museum, a security guard begs for mercy from a towering figure in silver armor. But he only gets a chilling reply: "I'm afraid my condition has left me cold to your pleas."

Mr. Freeze fires his weapon and a blue beam of cryonic energy surrounds the guard. He becomes frozen solid in ice. "Copsicle," the criminal coldly jokes.

Freeze's drilling truck pokes through the huge entrance. He has turned the inside of the museum into a frozen wasteland. Exhibits are covered in snow, the floor is slick with ice.

The villain approaches a cold-shattered exhibit case containing the Great White Diamond. Freeze grabs the diamond and holds it over his head, where it glistens like a star.

Suddenly, the skylight above the villain explodes in a shower of glass. A dark, bat-shaped form free-falls into the room, slides down the neck of a brontosaur exhibit, and drop-kicks directly into Mr. Freeze. The villain is stunned. The diamond flies out of his hand.

"Batman! You're not sending me to the cooler!" says Freeze, aiming his freezing gun at the Dark

Knight. But then Robin, Batman's faithful partner, bursts into the room on the Redbird. When Freeze turns to look, Batman kicks the cryo-gun out of the villain's hand. Robin soars over Freeze and kicks the weapon farther away—onto a high altar on the other side of the museum hall. "Score! And the crowd goes wild," yells the young hero.

Robin slides his bike to a halt and a group of Mr. Freeze's Icemen, wearing hockey masks and brandishing hockey sticks as weapons, advance on the crime fighters. "A hockey team full of goons," says Robin.

Batman and Robin press buttons in their utility belts and skate blades pop out from the bottoms of their boots. They skate to the Icemen and quickly relieve them of their hockey sticks. Then the heroes use the Icemen's own weapons to trip them up.

Meanwhile, Freeze tackles his way through a group of security guards and seizes his cryo-gun. He fires it to form an ice bridge. He slides smoothly down the bridge and away from the altar. Batman spots the cold criminal and tells his partner: "You get the diamond. I'll get Mr. Freeze."

Robin skates toward Freeze's thugs and checks them out of his way like a pro hockey player. He swoops down and scoops up the fallen gem.

Mr. Freeze runs behind the brontosaur and freezes its massive legs. With a shove, he topples the exhibit toward Batman and Robin. But the duo skates fast to avoid the falling dinosaur. It smashes into bits and pieces at their feet. "Well, that's definitely extinct," quips Robin.

One of Freeze's Icemen skates in from nowhere and knocks the diamond out of Robin's hand. And another Iceman hits the gem with his stick to send it toward the truck. Before the heroes can go after it, an entire group of Icemen rush in to block them. Thinking quickly, the duo pull two flagpoles down—as if they are about to joust. But instead they jam the flagpoles into the frozen floor and use them as pole vaults to leap easily over the henchmen.

The heroes land inches from the gem. But then another Iceman slapshots the diamond right into Freeze's waiting hand. "Thanks for playing," the villain says as he drops into the cab of his truck.

"Get the thugs. I'll get Freeze," Batman tells Robin. Then the Dark Knight leaps onto the truck's closing hatch.

As Batman drops inside, a tremendous roar rocks the cab of the truck. It blasts away from the rest of the vehicle and rises in the air like a rocket. Caught off guard by the blast, the hero is slammed into the bulkhead by Mr. Freeze. The villain holds Batman down as he freezes the hero's wrists and ankles to the wall.

Robin sees the capsule taking off and nimbly swings himself onto its side. He holds on to a porthole ledge for dear life as the capsule blows through the museum's roof and rockets toward the starry sky.

Inside the capsule, Batman tries to reason with Mr. Freeze. "You were a great scientist once. Don't waste your genius on evil."

Mr. Freeze ignores him and points to the capsule's altimeter, a device that measures distance above sea level. It reads 10,000 feet. "Watch the numbers, Batman. At 30,000 feet your heart will freeze and beat no more."

The altimeter jumps to 15,000 feet.

"After you have frozen, your icy tomb will plummet back to Gotham City," says Freeze as he steps into a glide-wing backpack mounted on the wall.

"That will slaughter thousands."

"Ain't it grand. Freeze well, Batman."

Freeze opens the door to the capsule and jumps out. He plummets toward Gotham City—until a sleek wing extends from his backpack and allows him to glide gently down like a snowflake.

Robin jumps into the freezing capsule through the open hatch. But Batman seems disappointed: "I thought you were going to stay in the museum and round up the thugs."

As he pulls a laser from his Utility Belt to free his partner, Robin replies: "How about: 'Nice to see you.' 'Glad you're here to save my life.'"

As his ice shackles melt, the Dark Knight lectures his friend: "When we get home we're having a little communication workshop."

Batman checks the altimeter: 20,000. "We have to make sure this rocket doesn't turn Gotham into a crater." Batman attaches a bat-shaped charge to the ceiling and activates it. It glows a bright green.

"Now what? Do we call a taxi?" says Robin.

The Dark Knight grabs a door handle marked CAUTION: EXPLOSIVE BOLTS. Robin understands and grabs a similar handle on the opposite metal door.

The duo pull the handles and leap onto the capsule doors as the explosive bolts blow them out into the sky.

Inside the capsule the Batcharge suddenly turns red. Above the free-falling heroes the capsule explodes into millions of pieces.

The heroes skyboard on the doors toward Mr. Freeze, who is gliding toward the skyscrapers of Gotham City. Batman closes in on the villain and pushes himself off his skyboard. He grabs Mr. Freeze around the

neck—causing the villain to drop the diamond!

Whirling smoothly through the air, Robin maneuvers himself under the falling gem and catches it!

Meanwhile, Freeze releases his glide-pack buckle, dislodging the pack and Batman. The hero and the glide pack spin away from the villain.

Freeze descends toward a giant factory chimney. He fires his cryo-gun. The inside of the stack quickly becomes covered with snow and ice, allowing Freeze to slide smoothly down the chimney.

Batman and Robin maneuver themselves toward the chimney and follow right behind the villain. They tumble headfirst through layers of ice, then pull out Batgrapples and fire. The grapples hit and the tethers slow the heroes' descent.

"Cool," says Robin. "Can we do that again?"

At the end of the ride, the heroes find themselves in the factory's basement. They spot Freeze fleeing down a corridor. The villain fires his cryo-gun at the ceiling. The sprinkler system explodes with the intense cold, creating an instant blizzard.

"Watch out for the—" But before Batman can get out that last word, a blast of wind roars down the corridor, slamming into the heroes. They cover themselves as best they can with their capes and make their way into nearby passages, away from the freezing wind.

Still in pursuit, Batman heads for a boiler room. But Mr. Freeze is waiting around a corner. The villain slams a door hard into Batman's face. The hero tumbles forward, dazed.

Robin leaps in from the hallway, but Freeze sees him. He fires his cryo-gun and turns Batman's partner into a frozen statue. The villain happily plucks the Giant White Diamond from Robin's icy hand.

Just then, the wall explodes—Freeze's henchmen have driven the drilling truck beneath the entire city to rescue their polar boss.

Mr. Freeze stands before the Dark Knight and taunts him. "Can you be cold, Batman? You have 11 minutes to thaw the Bird or he will die. What will you do: Chase the villain or save the boy?"

The Dark Knight has little choice. Letting Mr. Freeze escape, Batman whips out a Batheater and carefully aims it at the ice around Robin. As the ice melts, a cloud of steam surrounds his defrosting partner. Soaked and dripping like a wet cat, Robin coughs and asks: "Did we get him?"

Deep in a South American jungle, scientist Dr. Pamela Isley speaks into a micro-recorder: "I still have high hopes for the animal-plant cross-breeding. If I can only find the correct dose of Venom, these plants will be able to fight like animals. I will have given flora a chance against the thoughtless ravages of humanity."

Suddenly, an agonized scream rips through the air, terrifying Dr. Isley. She runs toward the sound, which has come from behind a door that reads PROJECT GILGAMESH. She wonders in fear: "What is he doing in there?"

Just then the door opens. Startled, Dr. Isley drops her recorder. "Dr. Woodrue!"

"Dr. Isley, loveliest flower in our garden!" Woodrue, a woolly-haired scientist, moves up close to Isley. He backs her against a table and spies her latest experimental harvest. "What do we have here? A new supply of Venom!"

Isley is furious. "What are those screams? You have to tell me what you're doing with my Venom!"

Woodrue ignores her and, taking her Venom sample, goes back through the marked door. But before it

can close, Isley kicks her fallen recorder between the door and the jamb—stopping the door from shutting. She sneaks in—hearing the screams, which are growing louder.

Isley finds Woodrue standing before a gathering of generals, dictators, and other powerful figures. "Ladies and gentlemen," he is saying. "I give you the future of military conquest." Woodrue points to the scrawny prisoner shackled to a gurney. "May I present Antonio Diego, serial murderer serving life in prison."

Woodrue pours Isley's Venom into an injector pack strapped to the back of the gurney. He presses a control stud and the injector pack pumps the milky Venom into Diego's skull. The prisoner screams again and again! Then, suddenly, his chest begins to enlarge, his neck thickens, his arms expand like balloons.

"Behold! The ideal killing machine. I call him *Bane*. Imagine your own personal army of Bane soldiers. Bidding begins at a mere ten million dollars."

Woodrue continues to pump Venom into the prisoner. Diego grows even larger, his legs become like timber, and his chest and arms become so large that his shackles begin to snap. It is Isley's turn to scream.

Woodrue rudely grabs her and walks her back to her lab. "Join me," says Woodrue. "The two of us, entwined, side by side . . . "

"Join you?" says Isley. "When I get through, you won't be able to get a job teaching high school chemistry!"

"Well, I can respect your opinion, but sadly I'm not good at rejection." The woolly-haired madman shoves Isley back into the work tables. Plant samples and chemicals start raining down on her. He grabs shelves of cages and test tubes and beakers bubbling with hot Venom and smashes it all down on the helpless Isley . . . until her body lies silent and still.

Woodrue smiles and returns to his lab to begin the auction.

After their chilling encounter with Mr. Freeze, Batman and Robin—in their other identities as billionaire Bruce Wayne and his ward, Dick Grayson—warm up at their secret headquarters, the Batcave. Alfred, Bruce's lifelong butler, stands nearby, ready to attend to the heroes' needs.

While Dick shivers in a blanket, Bruce turns on a monitor and runs a video from Gotham University Labs two years past. On the screen is the man who would become Mr. Freeze.

"Dr. Victor Fries," says Bruce. "Two-time Olympic decathlete. Nobel Prize winner in molecular biology. After his wife contracted McGregor's Syndrome, he froze her in cryogenic sleep until he could find a cure."

On the video, alarms flash as Fries is caught in a explosion of cryogenic solution.

"Somehow he survived. But the solution mutated his body. Now he needs extreme cold to live. His cryo-suit uses diamond-enhanced lasers to keep him at zero degrees. And if it's ice the iceman wants . . . Alfred, we're going to need the Wayne diamonds."

"We're going to trap ourselves a snowman!" adds Dick.

Later, Alfred sits alone in his quarters. Looking pale and weak, he speaks into a tape recorder: "Still unable to reach you. Have vital information you must see."

In South America, Dr. Woodrue seals the deal to sell the Bane formula. As he hangs up the phone, a patch of ivy on the wall behind him slowly begins to move. Suddenly, the leaves rustle and a green figure bursts from beneath the brush: A beautiful woman in torn clothes, her hair a burning magenta, her skin a lush white, and her eyes a brilliantly deep green.

"Dr. Isley? You look great—though you're supposed to be dead."

"I've had a change of heart," says the scientist, kissing Woodrue. "The animal-plant toxins you dumped on me had an unusual effect," she continues.

"They replaced my blood with chlorophyll and filled my lips with poison."

Woodrue begins to choke and falls to his knees, clutching his throat.

The woman who is now Poison Ivy spills beakers of chemical onto the floor and then tips over a lit Bunsen burner. Flames burst into life and begin to consume the lab.

Just then Ivy spots a broken beaker. The logo on it reads WAYNE ENTERPRISES. The name plants an idea in Ivy's head.

She then releases the engorged Bane. Free from the cruel Dr. Woodrue, the silent strongman is eager to join the stunning villainess. "Come, Bane, darling," she says. "We've got a plane to catch."

The Snowy Cones Ice Cream factory has been closed for years, but it is the secret home base of one of Gotham City's most glacial villains—Mr. Freeze.

Freeze tells Frosty, his henchman, "Battling the Bat exhausted my power. But I was successful nevertheless." The villain holds up the diamond stolen from the Gotham Museum. "One more giant diamond and my freezing cannon will be complete. I will hold Gotham ransom. Unless the city bows to my demands, it will be winter here forever. They will have no choice but to give me the billions I need to complete my research, to find a cure for my wife."

Freeze enters a secret vault. Its sole occupant is a still form in a frozen coffin. There lies the villain's wife, Nora Fries, cold and alone and barely alive.

The doorbell rings at Wayne Manor and Dick rushes to open the door. He is surprised to find a beautiful young woman standing there.

"I'm so sorry to trouble you," she says. Just then Bruce and Alfred walk up behind Dick.

"Uncle Alfred!" shouts the young woman. Bruce and Dick are shocked. When did their Alfred become an uncle?!

Alfred seems delighted to see the young woman—Barbara Wilson. "My word," he says. "Has it really been two years since my last visit to England?"

"Two years, three months, four days. Roughly," replies Barbara.

Alfred explains to the bewildered Bruce and Dick that Barbara is the daughter of an old love of his, Margaret.

Later, as they tour the grounds of the Wayne Estate, Barbara tells the others that her parents were killed in an auto accident 10 years earlier. "Alfred has helped me out ever since."

"You have?" asked Bruce, surprised again at his old friend.

"Secrets are a virtual prerequisite in this house, don't you think?" replies Alfred.

Barbara explains that she is in on break from Oxbridge Academy—Alfred's alma mater—where she majors in computer science.

At the garage, Barbara seems fascinated by a particular motorcycle. "It's beautiful."

"It's a competition racer I've been fixing up," explains Dick excitedly. "Maybe one day I'll show you how to ride."

"I hope you'll stay with us," adds Bruce.

Eyeing the bike, Barbara agrees. "I'd love to stay."

Later, Barbara visits Alfred in his quarters. Only then does she notice how weak and pale he looks. But she does not mention it to the man who has been like family to her.

Alfred tells her how he has been looking for his brother Wilfred, with no success. "He is a butler in India. As one grows older, one yearns for family."

Barbara glances at a photo on Alfred's desk. It is of her mother. The inscription reads: "All my love, Peg."

"Peg?" she asks.

"My nickname for sweet Margaret," replies Alfred.

Barbara smiles. "It's good to see you again, Uncle. I've missed you."

"As I've missed you," says Alfred. "Sleep well, child."

But Barbara does not go to bed right away. She sneaks out of her room and back to the Wayne garage. Climbing onto the competition bike—the one that Dick is so proud of—she pulls a helmet from her backpack. She kick-starts the engine and rides like a demon toward Gotham City.

At the Gotham Observatory, Bruce Wayne is making a dedication speech for a new telescope. His lovely girlfriend, Julie Madison, stands proudly next to him.

"My father once told me that to succeed we need only pick our star and follow it. And so Wayne Enterprises is donating the world's most advanced telescope to the Gotham Observatory. Perhaps this telescope will give future generations a chance to find their own stars."

The new telescope will be able to see the sky above any place on Earth, but gossip reporter Gossip Gerty is more interested in Bruce Wayne's personal life. "Bruce, you and the exquisite Julie Madison have been going out forever. Are you planning to tie the knot?"

Wayne is flustered. "Get married? Me? No."

"No?" Julie is surprised.

"Um, I mean no plans at the moment," continues the red-faced Bruce.

"Bruce and I are lucky enough to be in love," says Julie. "And that is most certainly enough—for now."

As Julie goes off to tour the observatory, Dr. Pamela Isley enters—in a disguise that hides her distinctive hair and emerald eyes. She introduces herself to Bruce.

"What can I do for you, Dr. Isley?" says Bruce.

"I once worked for you. Or I did—at your facility in South America."

"We canceled our support for that lab. Dr. Woodrue was a lunatic."

"I see you knew him. Look here, Mr. Wayne, forget the stars. This Earth, our mother, our womb, she deserves our loyalty and protection."

"Actually, Dr. Isley, we're auctioning off a prize diamond to raise money for the Gotham Botanical Gardens. Just a few mammals doing what we can for our world's plants." Bruce hands her an invitation to the charity ball, not realizing that he is also inviting trouble for himself and Gotham City.

All the well-to-do citizens of Gotham gather that night at the Gotham Flower Ball at the Gotham Botanical Gardens. The Heart of Isis, a grapefruit-sized diamond owned by Bruce Wayne, is to be auctioned off. Elegantly dressed guests mingle and enjoy themselves. But two costumed guests are not there to party.

"You think Freeze will take the bait?" asks Robin.

"He'll be here," answers the Dark Knight.

The two of them do not take much note of the two costumed gorillas also milling around the gardens.

As Gossip Gerty begins the auction, one gorilla walks up to the stage and removes its costume. It is Poison Ivy, dressed flamboyantly in jade green tights and dark green gloves, boots, and tunic.

Robin smiles. "Gorilla my dreams."

Ivy lifts her green-gloved hands, which are filled with sparkling dust. She blows and the powder floats over the audience—including Batman and Robin. The chemicals in the dust mesmerize the patrons, making them all fall madly in love with Poison Ivy.

The villainess saunters through the gawking guests toward the entranced heroes.

"The name's Poison. Poison Ivy."

Batman cannot fight the dust's effect. He reaches for Ivy's hand and she lets him hold it. "Why not send Junior here to bed early?" says Ivy.

"On the other hand, youth does have its advantages." She turns to Robin and offers him her other hand—but not before blowing even more dust into the young hero's face. "Why settle for second place, Robin? With me, you'd be the star of the team."

The two spellbound heroes help Ivy onto the stage. She takes the Heart of Isis diamond and begins her own auction.

The men in the crowd, under a deep love spell, begin bidding for Poison Ivy! Even the Dark Knight bids: "One million dollars."

"Two millions dollars," says Robin, jumping in.

Batman whispers to him, "You don't have two million." And then he bids again. "Three million."

Robin whispers, "I'll borrow it from you," and then he bids, "Four million!"

Ivy is flattered. "You two boys aren't going to fight over little old me, are you?"

Suddenly, the entrance to the ballroom explodes. Something big and cold bursts through the door. Standing on top of his drilling truck, surrounded by swirls of cold air and hordes of his Icemen, is Mr. Freeze. He pulls out his cryo-gun. "Did I use the wrong door again?"

Reacting quickly, Batman hurls a Batarang to knock the weapon out of Freeze's hand. He and Robin rush toward Freeze, but they are surrounded by Icemen.

Meanwhile, Freeze smashes through security guards to get back his cryo gun. "All right, everyone chill." Freeze fires and turns the guests, the guards, and the flower arrangements into frozen statues. "I should have been a decorator."

The cool criminal climbs onto the stage to face Poison Ivy. "Let me guess," he says. "Plant Girl? Vine Lady? Miss Moss?"

"Actually," says Ivy, "Captain Cold, the name is Poison Ivy." And with that she blows a handful of dust at Freeze's face.

The cool villain laughs. "Pheromone dust? Doesn't work on the cold-hearted. Now, if you please," he says, extending his gloved hand.

Ivy is caught between ice and a cold place—she has no choice. She hands him the Heart of Isis.

Batman and Robin finally knock out the last of the Icemen and chase after Freeze. Outside in his ice truck, the villain is creating a frozen bridge to a giant statue, so he can escape. But the Batmobile and the Redbird are in close pursuit.

Batman realizes that Freeze is going to jump off the statue down to the rooftops below. He knows the Batmobile can make it, but the Redbird can't.

He radios Robin. "Pull back. You can't make the jump."

Stubborn, Robin rides on. "I can make it."

While the Batmobile shoots across the ice bridge and down the statue's arm, Batman accesses his on-board computer to disable Robin's motorcycle. The Redbird's engine suddenly stops and Batman's angry partner skids to a sharp halt.

Freeze's truck leaps off the statue and lands on a nearby sloping roof. The villain screeches to a stop and spins the truck around, pointing its cryo-gun directly at the Batmobile. Batman rockets his engine to make the jump—but in midair it is hit with the blast from the freeze gun.

Inside the Batmobile the controls freeze over. A monitor flashes SYSTEMS FAILURE. Batman has only one choice.

As the Batmobile continues to tumble down to a rooftop below, the Dark Knight explodes out of the icy windshield. He spins himself in the air—and lands right on top of Freeze's truck.

Mr. Freeze sees the shadow of the Bat descend upon him. "Uh-oh."

Batman smashes through the dome in the truck and pulls out a stunned Mr. Freeze. "I'm putting you on ice."

That night all is not well at Wayne Manor.

"I could have made the jump," says Dick.

"You could have splattered your brains on the side of a building."

"You know, when I was in the circus with the Flying Graysons, we were a team. We had to trust each other. That's what being a partner is all about. Sometimes counting on someone else is the only way to win."

"Your head isn't even on the job. All you could think about was Poison Ivy."

"You can't stand that she might have wanted me. You have to have everything, Bruce. This is no partnership. You're never going to trust me."

Dick walks off as his mentor and friend watches in silence.

Later, after another night out, Barbara sneaks the competition bike back into the manor's garage. Dick comes up behind her and touches her shoulder. Startled, she reacts quickly, flipping him over her shoulder. Dick lands with a embarrassing thud.

Barbara turns and realizes who it is. "Ooh, I'm so sorry," she says quickly. "Judo lessons. And I just *had* to take the bike out for a spin."

She leaves before Dick can speak. But Batman's young partner is suddenly more curious than ever about this new houseguest.

In a Gotham City back alley, two figures approach the Blossom Street Turkish Baths, an abandoned

building that is occupied by a group of young punks. The larger of the two figures easily smashes through the wooden boards over the door.

The punks inside do not like this intrusion. They surround the large, silent figure—Bane. But he quickly plows through the punks. They run away, grateful to still be alive.

Poison Ivy steps forward and looks around at the dusty interior. "Bane, let's redecorate."

Bane breaks open a water line and begins to irrigate the dirt floor. As Poison Ivy drops tiny plants into the moist ground, she says, "Bane, I've found a fellow who strikes my fancy. He's a cool customer, yes, but I detect a ruthless charm in him that I may be able to use to my advantage."

In Robin's private area of the Batcave, Dick Grayson stares at the computer monitor, at an image of Poison Ivy taken from a news photo.

At that moment an alarm sounds. The monitor's image switches to a security film; it shows Barbara climbing out of her window and down the outside wall of Wayne Manor. "Got you!" says Dick, smiling.

Barbara speeds into the night on the competition bike.

She rides to a Gotham City alley where groups of motorcycle gangs have gathered to race. Barbara

hands over the $250 entry fee. As she moves to the starting line with the others, one last helmeted racer emerges from the shadows to pay his entry fee.

The racers rev their engines. A pistol is fired and the riders take off wildly down the street.

Some go over the tops of cars, others across the tops of stoops. A biker next to Barbara careens into an exploding pile of trash cans.

A biker named Spike, Barbara, and two others take the lead, leaving the rest in the dust.

One of the leading bikers hits an oil skid and spins out of control. The race is down to three. Barbara, Spike, and the mysterious last entrant race toward an unfinished steel bridge. The finish line comes up fast—but just beyond the finish line the bridge ends. The trick is to cross the finish line first, *but not so fast that you go over the edge and into the water below.*

Spike falls out of position. It's Barbara against the mystery biker. Barbara can't see his face—she can't see that it's Dick Grayson.

The finish line comes up fast. But instead of braking, both bikers gun their engines.

Barbara flies over the finish line with Dick just behind her. Both are going too fast and shoot over the edge of the unfinished bridge, soaring into the air. Dick and his bike make it across to the road on the other side, but Barbara's front wheel hits the edge badly and she begins to roll backward. Suddenly, she and her bike slip over the edge.

Dick spins around and sees what's happening. He ditches his bike and leaps toward the edge. Dick's jump sends him too far over the lip. He manages to hold on using only one foot and catches Barbara by the ankle! As they dangle over the abyss, Dick says, "So this is where you hang out."

Later, Barbara collects her winnings and offers the money to Dick to replace the bike she lost.

"Keep it," he says.

"Of course, Dick Grayson, ward of the fabulously wealthy Bruce Wayne. Why would you need a few hundred dollars?"

"Hey, what's your problem?"

"I guess I'm not comfortable with the idle rich. Even when they try to act like heroes."

"Well, get comfortable fast. Because we only have one bike and it's a long walk home."

Back at Wayne Manor, Barbara tells Dick why she began racing. "After my parents died, there was something about the speed, the danger that took me out of myself, that made the hurt go away. You wouldn't understand."

Dick, whose own parents were killed by a sinister criminal, only replies, "You'd be surprised."

"I've won enough money at street racing to do what I've always dreamed. I'm going to pay back Alfred and liberate him from his dismal life of servitude."

"But Alfred and Bruce are like family. Alfred's happy here."

"You honestly don't know, do you? You can't even see what's in front of your own eyes. Alfred's very sick." With that, she disappears upstairs, leaving Dick even more confused.

At Arkham Asylum, where Gotham City's worst criminals are imprisoned, Mr. Freeze busily sculpts an

ice statue of his wife when a guard approaches him. "Hey, icehead, your sister's here to see you."

"Sister?" asks the villain.

Another guard enters, followed by a woman in a long cloak. The woman sheds her cloak to reveal her skintight green costume—it's Poison Ivy. The two guards can't help staring at her beauty.

She smiles at them. "What if I told you one kiss from me would kill you?"

The naive guards think she is joking and so they pucker up. She kisses one, then the other. Suddenly, both guards choke and fall to the ground.

"Impressive," notes Mr. Freeze.

Ivy gets right to business. "I'm here to set you free."

"And what does the lady want in return?"

"Let's cool it for now. There's someone I want you to meet."

Bane enters, wheeling in Freeze's armor. Freeze is surprised. "Ah, a laundry service that delivers."

Freeze dons his armor, but his power supply is dangerously low. "They've confiscated my generator diamonds. I'm running on empty."

The terrible trio hears guards approaching. Bane begins to smash the cell wall to escape. Freeze reaches for his holster. "No gun," he realizes. "How disarming."

"I wonder if I'll get a cell with a view of the gardens," sighs Ivy.

"My dear daisy, don't despair," says Mr. Freeze as he walks to a sink set into the wall of his cell. He turns on the water and then cracks the seal of his own glove to release the cryo-gas that protects him. He aims the gas at the spigot. Suddenly, the pipes around the room begin to freeze, bulging with cold. The frozen water splits the metal and the metal cracks the stone wall. Finally, the wall itself splits apart to reveal

night and the rushing river far below the asylum.

"While I get my diamonds, you will retrieve my wife."

"Hold it," says Ivy. "You never said anything about a wife."

Freeze insists. "You want to be partners. Then bring me my bride!"

"Okay, okay, where do I find her?"

As the cell door breaks open with the force of the guards' blows, the newly united villains jump toward the rushing waters.

Bruce walks with Alfred through Wayne Manor, shutting out lights for the night.

"Are you well, old friend?" asks Bruce.

"As well as can be expected," replies the butler.

"Tell me, have you ever regretted working here, Alfred?"

"Attending to heroes, no sir. My only regret is that I was never able to be out there with you."

"Not all heroes wear masks, my friend."

Alfred smiles, but the warm moment between the two is broken when Dick runs in with some cold news. "Freeze has escaped."

Outside the Snowy Cones Ice Cream factory, Police Commissioner Gordon shows Batman and Robin surveillance photos of Freeze, Ivy, and Bane escaping from Arkham.

"Poison Ivy?" wonders Batman. "Why would she help Freeze to escape?"

Batman and Robin explore the building and discover a walk-in freezer. Batman examines the cache of food inside it and

then lifts a frozen Oriental dinner. Suddenly, a secret door to the secret vault swings open.

"How did you know?" asks Robin.

"Open Sesame . . . Chicken."

Inside the vault, they find Nora Fries in her coffin. Batman checks a nearby monitor. "She's still alive. He's even found a cure for the early stages of McGregor's Syndrome."

"Can he save her?"

"No, her case is too advanced. But maybe someday, with more research, he will."

At that moment spirals of Ivy's sparkling love dust begin winding through the room. Batman and Robin follow the dust to a passage and two service doors. They open the doors and find not Poison Ivy, but the Venom-pumped Bane.

Robin rushes at Bane, but the villain sideswipes the hero, sending him flying off the stairs.

Robin just misses falling into a giant vat of ice cream. Standing up, he finds himself face-to-face with Poison Ivy.

Meanwhile, Mr. Freeze enters the factory and surprises Gordon and his officers. The cold criminal pulls a lever marked COOLANT GAS. Vents around the room hiss and blue cryo-gas begins to escape. Freeze smashes through the policemen as they slip on the fast-freezing floor.

"Hey, pretty birdie," says Ivy, as she blows a pile of dust into Robin's face. She comes closer, leaning toward the dazed hero's face. "Polly want a kiss?"

But Robin looks up to see Bane pummeling Batman on the catwalk. He races to join the fight.

"I must be losing my touch," says an annoyed Ivy.

Bane kicks Batman off the end of the catwalk as Robin leaps on top of the villain. Now the Dark Knight finds himself face-to-face with Poison Ivy. She blows a huge handful of dust into his face. She licks her lips and leans in for the kiss. But at the last second, Batman averts his face. Fighting the effect of the dust with all his will, Batman tells her, "You're going to jail."

"I'm a lover, not a fighter," says Ivy, smiling coyly. "That's why every Poison Ivy action figure comes complete with *him*." She points and Batman whirls around to see Bane—with Robin unconscious at the villain's feet.

Back in his diamond vault, Freeze opens a safe and fills his armor's power compartments with diamonds. His usual pale color returns. "Ahh, chilled to perfection." Freeze hits a button on his watch and he is suddenly encased in a shield of ice. Bullets bounce off him as he walks toward his weapons locker.

Elsewhere, Bane throws Batman into a wall. The huge villain slowly approaches the dazed crusader. Batman coils his muscles and launches himself at Bane. The silent villain is sent sprawling.

Meanwhile, Ivy closes in on Robin. "Stop living in the shadow of the big, bad Bat. You don't need him. You deserve your own bright shining signal in the sky. Let me guide you. Let me kiss you."

Just as he is about to plant a kiss, a tiny Batarang hits Robin's cheek.

It's from Batman, who asks his partner, "Why is she so desperate to kiss us? I'm betting her lips are poison."

Robin doesn't believe this and advances on his partner. "A poison kiss? You have some real issues with women, you know that? You couldn't stand that she was about to kiss me. You couldn't stand that something might be mine and not yours, could you?!"

Robin shoves Batman into a wall. In frustration Batman delivers a merciful but effective roundhouse punch, sending Robin into a vat of pistachio ice cream.

Robin refuses Batman's help. "Ivy's right. I don't need you. I'm going solo."

Batman looks around for Bane and Ivy but they are gone.

At that moment, in Freeze's secret vault, Ivy has found Nora Fries. "Sorry, Mrs. Freeze, I'm not good with competition." With a heart colder than her new ally's, Ivy pulls the coffin's plug.

Later, at the Blossom Street Turkish Baths, the vine-loving villainess tells Freeze that *Batman* deactivated his wife's coffin. "She's dead."

Freeze is livid. He swears revenge on the heroes. "Their bones will turn to ice. Their blood will freeze in my hands!"

"Kill Batman and Robin. Of course. But why stop there?"

"Yes, I will also take their precious Gotham. I will blanket the city in endless winter. First Gotham, then the world."

"Just what I had in mind," says Ivy. "A chance for Earth to start over again. Behold the dawn of a new

age." From a canister labeled PROJECT GILGAMESH, Ivy removes savage plants with hissing fangs. "I have created a race of plants with the strength of the deadliest animals. Once we have frozen Earth, these mutants will overrun the planet. And we shall rule them."

"You will distract the Bat and the Bird while I prepare to freeze Gotham."

"Can't we just ice them like everyone else?"

"Batman must watch his beloved Gotham perish."

"As a team the duncely duo protect each other," notes Ivy. "But Robin is young, impulsive. If I could get him alone . . . "

"But how best to bait a bird?"

"The way to a boy's heart is through his ego. How could he resist his very own *signal*?"

At Wayne Manor a doctor has examined Alfred and informs Barbara and Dick that the butler has Stage One of McGregor's Syndrome. *Alfred is dying.*

In the butler's quarters, Bruce tries to comfort his old friend. "Everything I've done," says Bruce, "everything I'm capable of and I can't save you."

"Everyone dies, master Bruce. There's no defeat in that. Victory comes in defending what we know is right while we still live."

"I love you, old man."

"I love you, too."

Later, the doorbell rings, and Dick and Bruce both go to answer it.

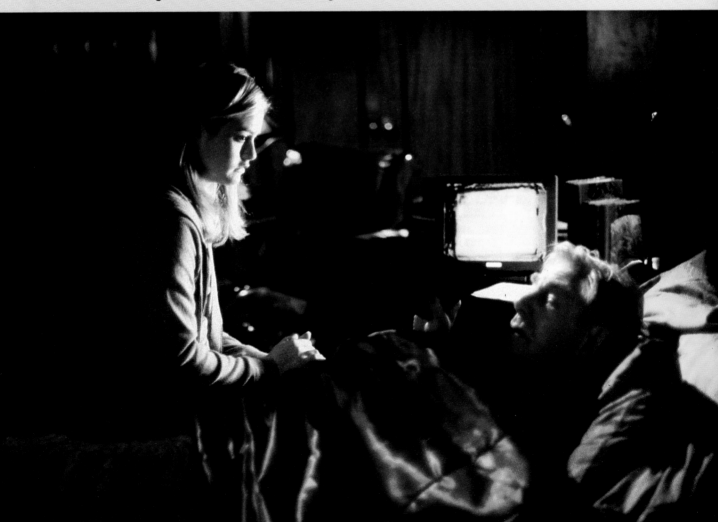

"McGregor's Syndrome," says Dick as they approach the door. "That's what Freeze's wife had."

"Yes, but Alfred's condition is less severe. Freeze's research says he cured a case like Alfred's. It just doesn't say how. I'm late for the telescope dedication. Then I'm going after Freeze and Ivy—alone."

"I'm going with you!"

"Dick, don't push me right now."

"Or what? No one can capture Ivy but the big, bad Bat! You just want her for yourself."

"Yes, you're right. That's the point. She's done something to us, got us fighting over her somehow. She's clouded your mind. You're not thinking right."

"But I am. For the first time. I'm tired of living in your shadow."

Dick walks away, leaving Bruce to answer the door.

It's Julie. "I've been ringing forever."

Barbara keeps Alfred company in his quarters. "I'm so sorry," she tells him, "I was too late to take you away from this place, to give you a chance to live your own life."

"Oh, no, child," replies Alfred, "I have been part of the greatest adventure ever known. I have found purpose here and a family I could never have found elsewhere."

Alfred smiles, but then he is hit by a sudden wave of pain. "Child," he tells Barbara, "you must do something for me. Find my brother Wilfred and give him this." He hands her a thick envelope. "I have duties he must fulfill in my stead. Only family can be trusted."

"What is it?"

"It is a sacred trust. Take it, child. But, I implore you: Never open it." With that, Alfred fades into sleep.

At the Gotham Observatory, Gothamites celebrate the unveiling of the new telescope. Pamela Isley—alias Poison Ivy—is disguised in a dull outfit, so as not to bring any special attention to herself. She begins what appears to be an idle chat with Commissioner Gordon.

"I've always wondered—where does that big bat light come from," she says, and as she speaks she opens a compact and blows a pile of love dust into Gordon's face. Some of the dust also hits Bruce Wayne, who is standing only a few feet away.

Gordon is instantly lovestruck. "It's on top of police headquarters. I have the keys right here in my pocket."

Isley gets very close to Gordon, so close that he does not notice her lifting the keys from his jacket pocket. "On second thought, you're too old for me," she says, and walks away from the rejected Commissioner.

As she tries to slip away, Bruce grabs her by the hand. He does not realize that she is one of his deadliest enemies.

"Dr. Isley. You're so enchanting tonight, the most beautiful woman I've ever seen."

Julie Madison is nearby and is amazed by what she is witnessing. "Bruce, what are you doing?"

Isley answers, "I think he's asking me on a date, in an awkward, stammering sort of way."

"You're asking another woman out when I'm right here?"

"I am? . . . I guess I am."

"Make a choice," demands Julie. "Her or me."

"Well . . . um . . . her."

"You've made your point. Good-bye, Bruce Wayne." With that, Julie turns on her heels and is gone.

But Bruce is still concentrating on Isley. "So, how about dinner?" But Isley ignores him and is quickly out the door, leaving Bruce brokenhearted and baffled.

At Wayne Manor, Barbara is overcome with frustration. She stares for a long time at the envelope in her hand. She has been trying for hours on her computer to find Alfred's brother, but without luck.

"Alfred said only family can be trusted. I'm his family, too." She opens the envelope and finds a microcassette and a CD-ROM. "And something inside me tells me that I need to find out what's on this disc now."

In Alfred's quarters, Bruce stares at his lifelong butler and friend hooked up to a life-support machine.

Unsure of what to do next, the man known as the Dark Knight enters the Batcave.

"Alfred, old friend, I could use your help right now."

"Right here, sir."

Stunned, Bruce spins. A computer monitor flashes the words COMPUTER SIMULATION under a three-dimensional image of Alfred.

The simulation speaks in Alfred's voice: "I anticipated the moment might arrive when I became incapacitated. As such, I programmed the Batcomputer to create this virtual simulation."

"It's good to see you," admits Bruce.

"What seems to be the problem?"

"Poison Ivy. First, she had an intoxicating effect on both Dick and me. Tonight, I found those feelings spreading to someone else."

"Specify, please."

"Dr. Pamela Isley. She used to work for Wayne Enterprises. Find a file with her photo."

A spinning image of Isley appears on the monitor.

"What was her area of research?" asks Bruce.

The computer Alfred replies: "Advanced botany. DNA splicing. Pheromone extraction."

"Hmm. Find the photo of Ivy after the flower ball."

An image of Ivy appears on the monitor beside the image of Isley. They are the same woman. "Amazing what a good wig and contact lenses will do," says Bruce.

Suddenly, an alarm sounds.

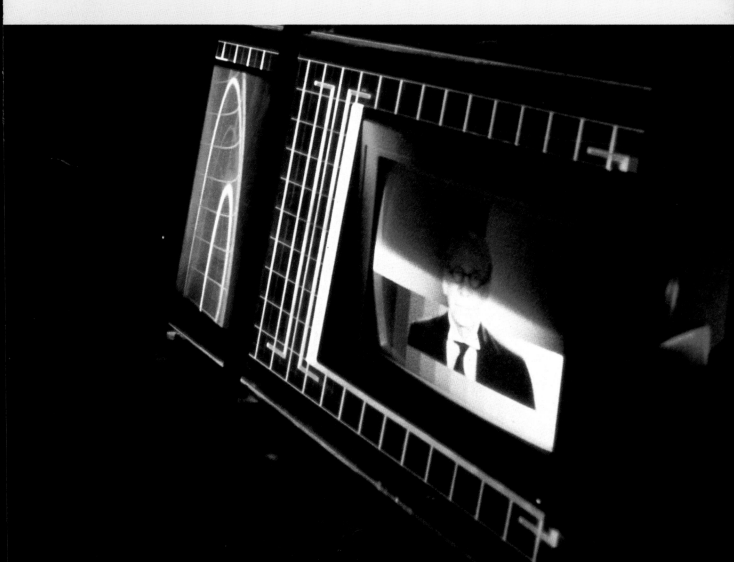

"What is it, Alfred?"

"It appears that someone has stolen the Bat-Signal."

In her room, Barbara uses her laptop to try to access the CD-ROM. But the disk is protected by a password. She guesses again and again—what word would Alfred use? Then suddenly she remembers. It's so obvious. She types in "P-E-G."

The file finally opens, revealing designs, blueprints, and incredible secrets.

"Oh my god."

In the sky above a new beacon shines—not the familiar Bat-Signal, but a bright red beacon. The shape within is not a bat, but a bird—the symbol for Robin.

At the Batcave, Robin recognizes his symbol. "That's not a batlight, it's a birdcall."

Batman comes up behind him. "Poison Ivy is really Pamela Isley. She must have stolen the keys from Gordon and altered the signal."

"And she did it all for me, for love."

"She infected us with some pheromone extract. She wants to kill you."

Robin can't believe this. "You'd say anything to keep her for yourself."

"You once said that being part of a team means trusting your partner. That sometimes counting on someone else is the only way to win. I'm asking you now, friend, partner, brother—will you trust me?"

Mr. Freeze and Bane have just smashed through the door of the Gotham Observatory. Freeze holds his cryo-gun on two scientists, while Bane begins setting explosive charges all over the room and around the giant telescope.

"Who is this nutball?" one scientist asks the other.

"That's Mr. Nutball to you," says Freeze, firing his cryo-gun. The two scientists turn to statues frozen in fear.

"If revenge is a dish best served cold," says Freeze, "then put on your Sunday finest. It's time to feast." The cold villain engages the icing engine he has invented, attaching it to the telescope. It begins to glow with a wave of blue cryonic energy. The blue wave spreads icily through the telescope and over the building. The nearby banks of Gotham River turn frosty white and the river itself freezes into an icy channel.

The observatory has been transformed into a fortress of ice.

Back at the Batcave, a small figure, new to its darkness and deep secrets, stands alone. The Batcomputer, sensing her motion, flicks on the lights.

"Uncle Alfred?" asks Barbara Wilson.

"In spirit only," says the computer.

Walking to the console, she tells the simulation: "I think the boys need help."

She inserts a disc into the computer and "Alfred" tells her, "Your mother would be proud. Now forgive my being personal, dear, but I must know your size."

Robin follows the red signal in the sky to the Blossom Street Turkish Baths. The stolen signal is chained to the front door.

Inside, it is as humid as a hothouse. From the shadows, Robin sees giant flowers and fruits bursting with color. In the center of it all is a giant bed of buds where Poison Ivy waits.

"I'm glad you came."

"I want us to be together," replies Robin, getting closer. "But I need to know you're serious about turning over a new leaf. Tell me your plan."

"Kiss me and I'll tell you."

"Tell me and I'll kiss you."

"Very well," sighs Ivy. "Freeze has turned the new telescope at Gotham Observatory into a freezing cannon. He's about to turn the city into a big ice cube."

"I've got to stop him," Robin says, about to walk away.

Ivy pulls him back to her. "One kiss for luck."

Robin can't resist. They kiss and Ivy smiles. She says, "Bad luck, birdie. It's time to die."

"What do you mean?"

"You should have listened to your pointy-eared pal. These lips can be murder."

"Then you never loved me?" asks Robin.

"Love you? My only joy is knowing my poison kiss is sucking the life from your apelike face."

"I'm not going to say I told you so," says another voice from the shadows.

Ivy spins. From the darkness a tall figure emerges. Batman.

"You're too late."

"Sorry to disappoint you," says Robin. "But rubber lips are immune to your charms." As he peels a rubber coating from his mouth, Ivy becomes green with anger.

"Robin and I found the cure to your evil spell. That's teamwork."

Screaming in rage, Ivy shoves Robin into a lily pool, where he is immediately tangled in predatory vines.

Vines above Batman grab him and hang him upside down. The incredibly strong plants begin to squeeze the life out of the heroes.

"My vines seem to have a little crush on you two. Gotta run."

Suddenly, the skylight above the villainess explodes in a shower of glass. A dark, bat-shaped form free-falls into the room.

It's a woman—in a skintight bat costume. "Poison Ivy, you're about to become compost."

Taking advantage of the distraction, Batman pulls out a Batknife and begins to cut himself free. Meanwhile, Robin struggles to disentangle himself from the water vines.

The woman in the bat costume begins a martial arts battle with Ivy. "Chicks like you give women a bad name."

But Ivy gets the upper hand and backs the new heroine against a wall. "As I told the Lady Freeze when I pulled her plug, this is a one-woman show."

"I don't think so." The heroine grabs Ivy's hair and knocks her out with a hard knee to the forehead.

Free from the vines, Batman drops down as Robin finally pulls himself out of the pool.

Batman begins the introductions. "And you are?"

"Batgirl."

"Batgirl?!" says Robin. "Not Batwoman? Batperson?"

"It's me, Barbara. I found the cave!"

"You know who we are," says Batman.

"We have got to get those locks changed," adds Robin.

Out of the darkness three powerful vehicles speed toward the Gotham Observatory.

At the helm of a sleek, one-man sail is Robin. The Batsled slides across the frozen water of Gotham River.

Moving beside him is a white Batmobile on rocket skis, the Bathammer—driven by Batman.

And falling into line with them is the Batblade, a single-bladed rocket snowcycle ridden by Batgirl.

Upriver at the frozen observatory, Mr. Freeze spots the Batvehicles. "Ivy failed to stop them. And it appears that the duo is now a trio. No matter. Watch, Batman, as your beloved city freezes."

Freeze points the telescope at downtown Gotham and fires. People walking their dogs, friends hanging out on stoops, others at work, in their cars, in their homes are all frozen solid. Mailboxes, lampposts, the pavement itself, all become covered in glistening ice.

Meanwhile, on the frozen river, Freeze's Icemen begin as assault on the heroes.

Batman radios his partners. "Attack Plan Alpha."

"Alpha, roger," answers Robin.

"Somebody want to tell me what Attack Plan Alpha is?" asks Batgirl.

"Divide and conquer," replies Robin.

On Freeze's truck, Icemen launch rockets at the Bathammer, blowing holes in the icy river. Batman maneuvers around the rockets and aims straight for the speeding truck. He shoots two torpedoes at the frozen river. The ice explodes, creating a huge hole in front of the truck. The driver can not swerve in time and dives in. Batman allows himself a quick joke, "Don't sink and drive."

Meanwhile Robin pulls the boom on the Batsled. The sail puffs and he changes course. The two Icemen skiing toward him collide and fly into the ice.

Batgirl hits a display panel on the Batblade and selects a setting called Ice Cutter. The front scythe peels back to reveal a sharper blade. She uses her deft driving skills to spin and skid, sending a wave of chopped ice into the faces of the Icemen. Temporarily blinded, they topple over. "That's what I call a close shave," she says.

Mr. Freeze sees the Bat-team advancing. "Time you cooled your heels." He fires at the frozen channel ahead of the Battalion. A giant wall of rock-hard ice forms, blocking the river.

Batman hits a console stud marked *Emergency Burn*. The Bathammer's engine roars and the Bathammer blows straight through the wall in an explosion of ice.

Robin and Batgirl neatly shoot up the face of the ice wall and land safely on either side of the Bathammer.

Freeze stares in disbelief. He turns to Bane. "As they say in show business, you're on. Take the boys and get the kids. But bring me the big bat."

Batman checks the clock at Gotham Tower; it reads 11:49. "We have less than 11 minutes to stop Freeze and thaw the city."

The three heroes climb the icy cliff to the observatory. On the icy ledge a score of Icemen attacks. Batman reaches for his Batarang, but then decides, "Let's do it the old-fashioned way." A roundhouse here. A jab there. And the thugs go down.

Confronted by armed Icemen, Robin spots a heavy overhang of snow above the thugs. Bringing his hands together, Robin yells at the top of his lungs. An avalanche of snow collapses on the Icemen, burying them.

Batgirl calls out each blow as she takes out the rest of the thugs—with a kick—"Pow!"—a punch—"Wham!"—and a backhanded strike—"Kazow!"

"No sign of the snowman," says Batman as the team enters the observatory.

"Maybe he melted," adds Robin.

Batman climbs up the telescope platform and uses Batcharges to begin defrosting the two frozen scientists.

"Batman, we have eight more minutes," reports Robin.

"Sunlight could reverse the freezing process."

Batgirl notes, "But sunrise isn't for five hours."

"Not here," says Batman.

"But it's morning in the Congo," adds Robin.

Batman points to a monitor showing the placement of satellites in orbit. "If we could relay the sunlight from the other side of the equator . . ."

"It takes the satellites about a minute to re-align," says Batgirl, then she notices two small mirrors on the telescope barrel covered in ice. "But, look, those targeting mirrors are frozen. The sun beam idea won't work."

Batman tells the others to thaw the mirrors while he uses the computer to re-align the satellites. Using their lasers Robin and Batgirl begin defrosting the mirrors on the telescope barrel.

As Batman types in the re-alignment commands, the satellites in space fire their thrusters and their mirrors slowly begin to turn. The plan is working. •

A clock in the room reads 11:54. Batman works on the telescope, but suddenly Mr. Freeze is there. "Tonight's forecast—a freeze is coming!"

Freeze grabs Batman and hurls him up over his head. Then the villain yanks the telescope's control joystick—causing the telescope to tilt sharply downward.

When the barrel tilts, it sends Robin and Batgirl down toward the front lens. From there it's a long drop to the city below.

Batman sees Freeze climb toward the controls and his two partners rolling toward the abyss. He knows he can't save them *and* stop the villain.

With little choice, he rushes toward Freeze just as Freeze disables the target lock on the telescope. In space, the thrusters stop. The clocks in Gotham read 11:56. The heroes have less than four minutes to save the city.

Freeze pulls a control lever and the telescope begins to spin wildly. Batman slips and hangs from the telescope frame.

Outside, Batgirl rolls off the barrel and plummets toward the city. Robin rolls just a few feet behind her. He fires a Batgrapple over his head. His grapple secures in ice and, as he falls, he reaches down for Batgirl.

58

Batman flips himself back on the spinning telescope, advancing on Freeze. "Millions will die so you can save on air-conditioning."

"We aim to freeze," says Freeze as he fires his cryo-gun.

Batman's suit's armor deflects the blast, but its force knocks him off the side of the scope. He catches himself, but hangs precariously off the side of the barrel.

Meanwhile, Freeze smashes the control joystick—causing the telescope to spin out of control. It crashes into a tower and Freeze is thrown by the impact. His cryo-gun falls. He scrambles for the weapon. But, suddenly, Batman looms above him.

Freeze whacks the Dark Knight into the wall, but the hero bounces back, hurling himself into the villain. The force of the blow knocks Freeze toward the back of the telescope.

The Dark Knight turns back to the console and types in the rest of the re-alignment commands. The satellites' mirrors open and begin to glow with sunlight. The clock reads 11:58.

Freeze screams as the light hits him. The villain leaps onto Batman. He lifts the Dark Knight over his head and hurls him down the telescope barrel— toward the opening in the roof and the city below.

Robin catches Batgirl just as she fires a Batgrapple from her wrist. Robin's tether pulls taught for a second, and he holds her dangling above Gotham. "I've got you," says the young hero.

But his grapple gives way and they both fall again.

But Batgirl's grapple hits the metal roof above them and holds firm. Her tether pulls taut and now she holds Robin dangling above Gotham. "No, I've got you."

The two scientists, now completely thawed out, see Batman tumble down the barrel.

"Wow, it's Batman."

Batman tells them, "Nice to meet you. Can you give me any more height on this thing?"

"Going up," says one scientist as the other one pulls an emergency lever. The telescope suddenly tilts straight up and Batman is sent soaring. He flips in midair and lands directly behind Freeze.

"You've turned Gotham to ice," says Batman delivering a crescent kick to the villain's midsection. "You've endangered countless lives." A double sidekick. "It's payback time."

But Freeze grabs Batman and chucks him over the side of the rail. Batman fires a Batarang and its cable loops around the platform railing—and Freeze's neck. Freeze lurches over the railing and his weight pulls Batman back up to the platform.

The mirrors overhead align and beams of sunlight strike the icing engine and Mr. Freeze. The

telescope activates and a powerful thawing beam shoots from its lens.

Batman turns to the withering Mr. Freeze. "You're losing your cool."

"I think not," says Freeze. "There'll be no hot time in the old town tonight." The villain presses a button on a remote control, causing all the charges laid by Bane to explode. The telescope tilts and drops out of the observatory's eye slot. It falls and explodes in the frozen river.

Batgirl and Robin finally climb safely onto a ledge. But then Batgirl notices a new presence. "Please tell me he's on our side."

Bane.

The silent strongman easily knocks Robin out of his way and advances on Batgirl. She tries to fend him off with a fast series of punches and kicks. But she might as well be hitting a steel wall.

Bane slams her into the ice and grabs her by the throat. Robin leaps up and rips the Venom-filled tubes leading from Bane's injector pack to his skull. The milky Venom sprays wildly in the air.

Bane collapses, writhing in the snow as the Venom effect is reversed. His thick muscles shrink, his giant chest sinks, his timberlike legs turn back to sticks. He is once again the scrawny Antonio Diego.

The two young heroes meet Batman back at the computer controls. Batgirl surveys the situation. "It's midnight. The telescope's gone. And there's no way to thaw Gotham City."

But Batman disagrees. "Theoretically, the satellites could be positioned to thaw the city directly. But it would take a computer genius."

Robin says, "I'm on it," and clears the rubble from the computer console. But the equipment seems dead.

"I'm on it," says Batgirl, as she nudges Robin aside and quickly patches together a few broken wires. The console lights up. She begins reprogramming the computer.

In space, the giant orbiting satellites re-align themselves. A bright disk of sunlight appears in one mirror, as is reflected from that one to the next and the next. Finally, the warm beam shines down on Gotham. The frozen observatory begins to thaw. The city begins to melt.

Batman walks over to Freeze, who lies amid the rubble, weak and gray with his rising temperature. Freeze struggles to speak. "Go on, kill me, just as you killed my wife."

"I didn't kill your wife." Batman presses a button on his Utility Belt and on his glove a tiny monitor plays an image of Poison Ivy. She is saying, "As I told the Lady Freeze when I pulled her plug, this is a one-woman show."

Freeze screams, his face streaming with frozen tears that resemble tiny diamonds.

"She's not dead, Victor," explains the Dark Knight. "We found her in time, restored her to cryogenic sleep. She's still frozen, Victor, alive, waiting for you to find a cure. Anyone with a gun can take a life. To give life, that's true power. A power you once had. I don't know if you'll ever find a cure for your wife, but I'm asking you now, Dr. Victor Fries, to save another life. Show me how to cure McGregor's Syndrome in the early stages. And maybe you can also save the man your wife once loved. He's still inside you, buried somewhere deep beneath the ice. Will you help me?"

Freeze stares at Batman. Finally he unseals his chest plate and removes two glowing pills. He holds them out, and with a bittersweet smile, says, "Take two of these and call me in the morning."

Morning finds the world's greatest crime-fighting team at Wayne Manor. Barbara, wearied by battle and worry, dozes on the couch, while an impatient Dick paces back and forth. Bruce stares out the window, aware that Freeze's cure may not work.

Suddenly, a throat clears, and Bruce turns to see Alfred, looking much healthier, descending the stairs.

Bruce rushes to meet him. "Alfred, are you . . . ?"

"I am quite well, it seems. Thanks to you all."

Batman hugs his old friend, and Barbara and Dick join in the family reunion.

Dick asks Bruce: "I have a question. When Batgirl and I rolled off the telescope, how come you didn't try and save us? It was the first time I fell and you weren't there to catch me."

"I knew you could handle it," says Bruce. At that Barbara clears her throat and Dick shoots her a glaring look.

"Sometimes counting on someone else is the only way to win," Bruce continues.

"But I captured Poison Ivy. Me, I did," Barbara chimes in.

"You're going back to school."

"You're never going to win this, Bruce," says Dick.

Barbara offers Bruce her hand: "Partners?"

Dick and Bruce put their hands on hers. "Partners."

Alfred smiles. "We're going to need a bigger cave."

That night, when the Bat-Signal appears in the sky above Gotham City, three costumed heroes race into the night to answer its call.